100% *Karma*

100% Karma

By Sirshree Tejparkhi

Copyright © Tejgyan Global Foundation
All Rights Reserved 2016

Tejgyan Global Foundation is a charitable organization
with its headquarters in Pune, India.

Published by WOW Publishings Pvt. Ltd., India

First edition published in June 2016

Second Reprint in November 2018

Copyrights are reserved with Tejgyan Global Foundation and publishing rights are vested exclusively with WOW Publishings Pvt. Ltd. This book is sold subject to the condition that it shall not by way of trade or otherwise, be lent, resold, hired out, or otherwise circulated without the publisher's prior written consent in any form of binding or cover other than that in which it is published and without a similar condition including this condition being imposed on the subsequent purchaser and without limiting the rights under copyright reserved above, no part of this publication may be reproduced, stored in or introduced into a retrieval system, or transmitted, in any form, or by any means, electronic, mechanical, photocopying, recording or otherwise, without the prior written permission of both the copyright owner and the above-mentioned publisher of this book. Any person who does any unauthorized act in relation to this publication may be liable to criminal prosecution and civil claims for damages.

Table of Contents

	Introduction	1
1.	What is Karma?	3
2.	From Doing to Being	10
3.	The Fruit of Karma	22
4.	The Law of Karma	27
5.	The Question of Rebirth	39
6.	Karma and Destiny	43
7.	Transcending the Three Temperaments	50
8.	Enlightenment through Conscious Karma	57

Introduction

The Ocean in a Drop

Who you assume as 'I' is a drop in the ocean;
Who you truly are is the ocean in a drop.

The knowledge of the ultimate truth of life is non-conceptual and cannot be expressed in words. It can be known only through direct first-hand experience. However, words can serve as pointers to recognize the Truth.

This book is like the Ocean in a drop. It presents the essential wisdom of life, which has been distilled from conversations between seekers and Sirshree.

This book is part of the 'Ocean in a Drop' series. It explains the crux of Karma and Karma-yoga, which are an important facet of life and its purpose. It throws light on the missing links in the understanding of Karma.

By reading these conversations, you will discover how to integrate the wisdom of Karma into practical living. The book reveals the Soul of Karma—the missing link in the practice of right action. Actions that are imbued with the Soul of Karma lead to completeness and fulfillment; they become 100% Karma.

These conversation transcripts help beginners in understanding the crux of action and its result, destiny and how to approach life's challenges. Advanced seekers of the ultimate truth of life can understand the deeper import of Karma-yoga and the art of conscious action through which liberation can be attained.

Every answer arises from the quintessence of wisdom. Scattered in these answers are 100 precious drops, which have been annotated for repeated reading 💧. Reading these profound drops of wisdom and contemplating upon them can bring about a paradigm shift in the perspective of life.

1

What is Karma?

Seeker 1: What is the real meaning of Karma? Is it different from action?

Sirshree: Every action is karma – thinking, looking, listening, sitting, standing, walking, running, driving. And every action begets its fruit. Inaction is also karma. If a student studies hard, he receives the fruit of hard work – he passes his exams with good scores. If a student does not study, he receives the fruit of his inaction as well – he may fail the exams. *Avoidance of action is also a form of action. Both, action and inaction are karma and beget results.*

You cannot escape karma. The journey of human life is perpetuated through karma. Understanding the essence of karma and following it up with awakened action is the way to enlightenment. Understanding is the key. When understanding is missing, one's karma can lead one astray.

Seeker 1: Very often, I avoid saying something that is the need of the situation. I avoid acting or decision-making to escape responsibility. From what you said, I understand that inaction is also karma. Escaping responsibility is also action. This is a shift of perspective for me. How can I perform awakened karma? How do I know whether my karma is right or wrong?

Sirshree: Your question about right karma expects a logical answer for what's right and wrong. The mind is comfortable when it is provided a clear list of do's and don'ts. *However, the truth of karma transcends both 'right' and 'wrong', it is beyond both 'doing' and 'non-doing'.*

The action that is considered appropriate in a given context can turn out to be inappropriate in another context. An act can prove to be benevolent or harmful, also depending on who is performing it.

Consider a man, who is inflicting pain on another with a knife. Now, would you consider this action right or wrong?

Seeker 1: Obviously it's wrong. Inflicting pain on someone is a crime.

Sirshree: Right. As you said, this is the 'obvious' answer. Let's go beyond the obvious and understand the context. What if it is a surgeon, who is using the knife to operate upon a patient? Is that a crime?

Seeker 1: Oh…No. In that case, the doctor is helping the patient.

Sirshree: What if the surgery was actually unnecessary and the doctor is only amassing wealth through unfair practices?

Seeker 1: Then it's inappropriate. In this case, doesn't the intention of the doctor determine whether the karma is right or wrong?

Sirshree: Yes… the intention behind the visible action is all-important. This throws light on an important missing link. *Mental actions, in the form of thoughts and feelings, are the primary determinant of the quality of karma, than the outward physical action.* The intention behind action determines whether the karma is appropriate. What may seem to be a terrible act to your eyes could possibly be backed by the purest intention. On the contrary, what may seem to be the most benevolent and kind act could be a crafted manifestation of a wicked intention.

Let's now consider that the doctor is virtuous and genuinely wants to heal the patient. But what if the doctor is performing the operation without adequate diagnosis? What if he is doing the surgery without being adequately informed about the patient's case? Will his karma be appropriate? What do the rest of you think?

Seeker 2: I feel that the doctor's act could prove to be inappropriate despite his best intentions. The treatment could be fatal. Knowledge of the case is important for right action.

Sirshree: Good. So we've seen that the aptness of karma is dependent on the intention behind the karma and the understanding of the context for karma. Now let's suppose that the benevolent doctor has carefully assessed the patient's case and carried out all the necessary diagnosis. However, he has had a bad morning on the day of surgery. He has had an argument with his wife and cursed his way through the traffic to the hospital. When he is at the operating table to do the surgery, his mind is clouded with anger and frustration. Does this change the quality of his karma?

Seeker 3: I think the quality of his action will depend on his ability to be focused. If the doctor is able to focus on the job at hand by setting aside his feelings, then it shouldn't matter. However, if his feelings get the better of him, it can affect his performance as a surgeon.

Sirshree: So the feeling that you bring into your actions also determines the quality of karma. *Pure feelings of compassion, oneness and gratitude that arise from an attitude of surrender to the divine will, transform work into worship.*

The Soul of Karma is embodied by these three aspects – love, understanding and pure feeling. Any act that is imbued with the feeling of love, wisdom, and pure virtuous intention is 100% karma. It arises from higher awareness. Action that arises from an awakened Soul of Karma brings completeness and fulfillment in your life.

Action arising from ignorance, lower intentions, devoid of love and compassion is soulless karma. It is reactive as it arises from the past conditioning of the mind. It does not give completeness. Far from being 100%, it entangles you and leads to sorrow or confusion.

Seeker 3: Isn't every action actually a reaction to situations? Is it possible to have pure non-reactive action?

Sirshree: Not all actions are reactions. Reactions are programmed responses to external or even internal stimuli. The subconscious mind has been designed to automate responses to certain stimuli.

Since childhood, we observe and learn certain fixed responses. The subconscious mind is the storehouse of such fixed responses.

For example, do you need to think twice before pulling your hand away from fire? Do you actually think, "This fire can burn my hand; let me take my hand away"? No. It happens automatically without conscious thought. The subconscious mind is programmed to enact this response to the stimulus of fire. We've borrowed this behaviour through genes, through our upbringing from parents, our neighbourhood, through school and largely through the media.

You suddenly brake the car to a halt when an obstacle appears on the road. You catch hold of anything you can get your hands on to when you stumble. These are automatic reactions. It's actually useful that your actions are automatic in these instances. It saves you the effort of consciously considering repetitive actions. This is indeed a blessing.

However, this blessing becomes a curse when it comes to programmed behaviour. For example, how is your response when you feel cornered in a group? Consider the compulsive need to withdraw from a scene where you sense insecurity or hostility. Consider the pleasure that is felt when the scene conforms to your liking. These deeply ingrained responses helplessly manifest, much against your conscious will.

Seeker 3: Yes... There are situations when I just can't control my response. I tend to respond impulsively. At times, when people speak harshly or swear, I feel agitated and retort at them. What is the relation between impulsiveness and Karma?

Sirshree: When someone speaks harshly or swears at you, perhaps you may be compelled to swear at them in return. When someone praises you, you may feel gratified and comply with their needs. You may say, "The situation was such, so I got angry." This is a reaction, because it is dependent on circumstances. Your behaviour with people is dependent on how they behave with you. You hand over the remote control of your life to people and situations. Most people lead life in this reactive way, by being a victim of their past conditioning.

Reactive living does not need higher awareness. You do not need awareness to follow the same beaten path every day. However, if you have to choose a new path, which is unknown, it needs awareness. *Creative living requires higher awareness. Human evolution is all about moving from reactive living to creative living; it is about raising the level of consciousness.* When you raise your level of consciousness, you begin to act less and less impulsively or compulsively. Your actions will become increasingly intuitive and creative.

Seeker 2: How can we act creatively in testing circumstances?

Sirshree: An awakened response arises intuitively from pure consciousness. It does not arise from the storehouse of programmed responses. It is fresh and creative. *Actions arising from pure consciousness are independent of prior mental conditioning. They are fresh and novel actions, free from past prejudices.* They are imbued with the Soul of Karma.

Develop the habit of questioning yourself in everyday situations. Ask yourself: "Am I reacting mechanically to this person, to this situation?" When you question yourself in this way, it creates an opportunity to respond creatively. With raised awareness, you become conscious of the space where you can choose your response.

When you practice being in the stillness of pure consciousness, your actions will arise from the freedom of choice of response. For example, if someone swears at you, you will choose an awakened response by either ignoring it or responding creatively. An awakened response is not constrained by fixed patterns of behaviour. The Soul of Karma awakens with rise in consciousness. Love, wisdom and pure feelings will drive your actions to attain completeness, making them 100% Karma.

Whenever you feel the need to act impulsively, take a pause and dip into the stillness beyond thoughts. This enables you to raise your awareness and take inspired action.

2

From Doing to Being

Seeker 1: We all are born, grow up, fulfill our responsibilities, have families and then pass away... What is the purpose of all this? What is the purpose of human life?

Sirshree: The purpose of life is 'life' itself.

When people are not prepared to receive higher answers, they are told, "The goal of life is to become a doctor, or an engineer, or just to be successful. If you want to become a carpenter, then become a good carpenter. If you aspire to become a doctor, become a good doctor."

Initially, such replies seem adequate. However, it is only when one is prepared to receive higher understanding that they get higher answers: *The goal of human life is that 'life should know life'.* Life, in this context, refers to the inner experience of aliveness within each one of us, which has been known as Self, God, Christ, *Ishwar*, *Allah*, Lord, and so on. It is the living consciousness within us due to which the body is alive and moving. In the absence of the enlivening consciousness, the body would be a mere corpse. The body moves only because of the presence of the Self, the conscious presence.

Let life return unto itself; let life experience its own essence. *When the life principle in a body is consciously aware of itself, it is called Self-realization. The purpose of life is to realize the Self and to be established in the Self.* Self here refers to God or Consciousness, the Source of everything, the very essence of life itself. 'The goal of life is life itself' means that the purpose of human life is to attain Self-realization and to be stabilized in that experience.

The underlying meaning behind this answer is that you should know yourself, your original nature. *It is only in order to realize who-you-truly-are and express its divine qualities that you have been associated with your body.*

When you know the real meaning of life, you will also understand the art of 'being life'. Many people wish to learn the art of living. But you don't have to learn the art of living; you need to learn the art of *being* life itself. This means that you have to shift your focus from the objects of perception to that which enables perception, from thought to that which enables thinking. You will then rise above the changing and limited to that which is changeless, eternal and boundless.

Up until now, you have lived your life assuming yourself to be a body. You identified yourself with your body and often said, "This person appreciated me; she made fun of me..." However, all this happened not with you, but with your body (the body-mind mechanism).

When you raise your level of consciousness to its pinnacle, you experience the inherent oneness of all beings and everything in the universe. The goal of life is to attain the experience of that oneness and be established in it.

When you are unaware of this whole-and-sole life purpose, you don't work at it. But when you gain clarity, you won't miss a single opportunity that helps you to progress further toward Self-realization.

Seeker 1: What exactly is Self-realization? Is it the ultimate goal of life? Isn't there anything beyond?

Sirshree: Self-realization is the realization of our oneness with Consciousness through experience of our true nature. We live by assuming ourselves to be our body and mind. When we experience our true nature as pure consciousness, beyond the body and mind, it is called Self-realization.

We live with the belief, "I am the body". When we clearly know the fallacy of this belief, the underlying oneness of everything is experientially revealed. The limited individual personality, that appears due to identification with the body, dissolves. The universal 'I', the real 'I' is realized.

Whatever we pursue in our worldly life is only the foreground. Self-realization is the background of all pursuits. It is the aim behind all aims of life, because it is the art of 'being' life itself. It is the fulfillment of the very purpose of human life.

Is there anything beyond Self-realization? It can be said that Self-realization is just the beginning. Self-stabilization is the ultimate goal.

There are many who experience momentary flashes of oneness when they are with nature or even in the midst of their daily lives. However, these are only samples of the experience of Self-realization, mere glimpses that happen when the understanding of our true nature shines forth.

Such glimpses of Self-realization are experienced when the judgmental mind momentarily becomes silent. But what happens after the glimpse? The judgmental mind emerges again and takes credit for the experience: "I performed meditation; I attained this deeply profound state; I experienced Self-realization." *The mind lacks the understanding that it cannot experience the Self. On the contrary, when the mind is stilled, the Self experiences itself.*

Self-stabilization happens when the comparing and judging aspect of the mind drops and no longer emerges. It is about permanently and constantly abiding in the experience of pure consciousness. One lives with the firm conviction of one's true nature beyond the body and mind. Self-realization without understanding is futile. It is meaningless to proclaim that you have attained Self-realization based on a one-time experience, without being permanently stabilized in that experience.

Self-stabilization is the ultimate purpose of life. If the body continues to indulge in old tendencies and habitual patterns even after many such glimpses of the Self, then the ultimate purpose is not served. The judgmental mind keeps returning with false beliefs and doubts about the experience of the Self. Due to this interference of the judging mind, the state of inner stillness in which the Self experiences itself remains veiled.

With Self-stabilization comes Self-expression – the expression of the Self through the body-mind mechanism. On attaining Self-stabilization at the age of thirty-five, the Buddha continued to spread the message of Truth till the ripe age of eighty. Siddhartha Gautama's body served as a medium for expression of the Buddha, the Self.

When the purpose of Self-stabilization is not clear, you might assume glimpses on the path as Self-realization and mistake that to be the ultimate goal. If Self-realization is seen as Self-stabilization, then that is the ultimate goal. If you see it as a one-time experience, then it is just the beginning.

Seeker 2: Can I behold God? How can I experience consciousness?

Sirshree: We live in a world where 'seeing is believing.' Hence, whatever is unseen or intangible is considered to be non-existent. Breeze is unseen, but the grass in the fields sways, proclaiming the presence of breeze. You conclude by inference that breeze exists, though you don't see it.

Suppose a child sees someone, completely veiled in a long cloak, walking down the street. He says, "See that empty cloak is walking." You would explain to the child that an empty cloak couldn't walk by itself. There has to be someone inside the cloak. The child may contend, "But I can't see anyone there." You would then explain, "Just because you are not able to see anyone there doesn't mean that there's no one."

The human body is like the cloak. God is the enlivening consciousness due to which the body comes alive. It is due to the enlivening consciousness that the body can walk, talk and act.

Expecting to behold God with your eyes is like trying to hear music with your eyes. Listening to music has nothing to do with eyes. You can never grasp anything that is non-visual with your eyes. *If you are expecting to see God, you need to understand that He is everywhere. Consciousness pervades the universe. It is the knowing principle that enables seeing. The existence of consciousness cannot be refuted because it is 'existence' itself.*

The mind wants to see God, but it should attain the understanding that God cannot be seen in terms of a defined physical reality. When the mind is infused with this understanding and develops faith in the existential nature of God, it surrenders its insistence to experience God or consciousness based on its own imaginations.

Once you experience God as the living consciousness within this body, it will be easy to recognize Him outside this body too. You will recognize God's presence as the all-pervading consciousness within all forms, both living and non-living. Myths and stories create a misconception that God incarnated only in certain bodies. But everyone and everything in the universe is His form alone.

The intuitive knowing that 'I exist', 'I am alive' is exactly the same within every body. It is this very experience of aliveness, which is the Source of everything. It is this Source that has been called 'God', 'Self', 'Lord', 'Allah', and so on.

Be it the body of a child or an adult, of man or woman, of a rich man or a poor man, this inner experience is the same. *This experience can be known only by being that, not by thinking about that, not by doing something.*

Seeker 2: How can I experience the divine presence without thinking or doing?

Sirshree: It is already being experienced every moment. It's just that you lack its recognition. The mind tries to understand it by imagining it.

Rene Descartes, a 17th century French philosopher once said, "I think, therefore I am." However, if existence were dependent on thinking, then we wouldn't exist if we stopped thinking. This is certainly not the case. When we are in deep sleep, we don't think but we continue to exist. We even comment on waking that we had sound sleep. We have to exist during deep sleep to be able to know that we did sleep well.

When the judging and reasoning mind drops, the experience of conscious presence is revealed. In that state, there's neither a need to think about it nor a necessity to do anything about it.

Understand this with an example. When someone is playing the piano, rendering a beautiful symphony, he is lost when the performance is at its peak. It is as if he does not exist then. The performer is lost in the performance. All that is happening is the performance. Where is the mind when this is happening? It has dropped for some time. But the mind comes back later and claims that it was present during the performance. The mind even takes credit for having been the 'doer' of the performance.

Musicians love to be lost in the peak of their performance. Athletes like being in the thick of activity. The real joy that they experience is because the mind drops and they touch the experience of conscious presence. However, they believe that it is the music performance or the athletic activity that is giving them joy. *The source of joy is not in the gross external world. True joy is the nature of your essential presence.*

A clear glimpse of our true nature can awaken us from our limiting beliefs and shift us onto this enlivening presence. *Presence or 'being' is the basis of existence. Presence comes first; thinking comes next; doing comes even later. To think or do, we have to first* be. *Being* or *Presence* is our true nature. Presence is independent of thought. Presence just *is*. It is the most obvious experience, the open secret – so open and obvious that we easily fail to notice it.

Seeker 2: You say that Presence just *is*. I gather that is some kind of stillness by nature. How can it then be the basis for thinking or doing?

Sirshree: Understand this with an analogy of the ocean and waves. Each wave is essentially the movement of the ocean itself. The existence of each wave is essentially the presence of the ocean. Waves do not have an individual existence or doership of their own… unless it is imagined to be so.

The wave is merely a form of expression of the ocean. But when the ocean identifies itself with this form of expression, it gives rise to an illusion of separateness, a notion of individuality. The wave assumes itself to be the doer. *Each human body-mind is a wave of expression of the Self. Bodies come and go, just as the waves rise and fall. But the Self, like the ocean, lives eternally and expresses incessantly through the human mechanism.*

The deeper part of the ocean exists as stillness, the state of Self-at-rest. This is unexpressed and changeless, existing beneath the changing surface. The state of Self-at-rest is pure consciousness, the state of nothingness with the potential of everything.

The ocean surface is dynamic; there is movement. Waves are the dance of the ocean; they are Self-in-action. At the surface, waves arise from the deeper stillness of the ocean and die down into it. Each body-mind is like a wave; Self is like the ocean.

When actions are seen from the standpoint of the stillness of presence, they are merely an expression of this divine presence. The waves are inseparable from the ocean; the ocean is the waves and also beyond the waves. It is the mind that sees the separateness of individual waves. The underlying presence sees itself through the seeing of the waves.

Know your being as the ocean, not as a wave; then you are out of the trap of mind; beyond doing and non-doing. With surrender of all action and doership itself, all thought and action are clearly seen as the spontaneous and passing rise and fall of waves on the surface of consciousness.

Clarity is experienced when the mind is transcended and understood as the play of waves on the surface of the ocean of pure consciousness. The waves then serve the purpose of Self-knowing instead of assuming an individual identity.

Seeker 2: So is the Self the doer or is it merely present?

Sirshree: Actions happen spontaneously owing to the presence of the Self. Take the example of the sun. All the affairs of the world happen in the presence of the sun. Flowers blossom in the presence of the sun. Human life is dependent on the sun. Man wakes up at sunrise and retires after sunset. But the sun does not wake anyone up, nor does it put anyone to sleep. It is merely present. *All activities happen owing to the presence of the sun. Similarly, everything happens owing to the enlivening presence of the Self. Life unfolds in this presence.*

Seeker 2: How can I *be* in presence?

Sirshree: The mind seeks fixed answers for 'how'. The experience of Presence is always available. If you try to check whether you are experiencing presence, you are trying to grasp it in your thoughts. *There is no need to try and grasp your presence through thoughts. You can either think about presence, or just be.* The experience of Presence is ever-present as the background of thoughts. It is the screen of awareness on which thoughts appear.

When you attempt to capture presence through thoughts, it eludes you. The mind insists, "I want to grasp this divine presence; I want to know how it is like." This wish becomes a hurdle in just being who-you-truly-are.

Suppose a soft sound is constantly playing in the background during the day. You would soon get used to it. After a few hours, you wouldn't even notice this sound, even though it continues to play. It's only when the sound stops momentarily that you become aware of its existence.

Similarly, the sense of presence has ceaselessly existed ever since your body was born. Your identity has changed – from being a child to becoming an adolescent, from being a youth to a middle- aged homemaker, from being a student to earning a living – but the sense of presence remains unchanged. If you were to take away all the roles that define you, you would still exist.

The song of presence is playing constantly; you *are* that. Being in this presence is the experience of pure joy, unconditional and boundless, independent of the world, untouched by situations.

You have been programmed to believe that you can gain happiness through whatever you do. You continue believing this without doubt because you see everyone else around you in the same pursuit. This makes you seek happiness in the world.

The world can never bring you lasting joy. Doing something cannot bring you joy. Action is not the means to joy. True action flows from joy. The real joy that is experienced in anything is actually the joy of presence.

Seeker 3: If we merely abide in Presence, what about the problems of daily life that have to be solved?

Sirshree: *Abiding in Presence does not amount to escaping from problems. On the contrary, being in Presence is the only true way of addressing problems. By being in presence, you need not solve problems. Rather, you will witness solutions arising from the problem situation itself.*

When you are away from your true nature of presence, the mind tends to give the problem undue importance by resisting it. Seeing the situation as a problem is the only problem. When you look at situations through the lens of your beliefs, you build resistance. Resistance causes the problem to persist.

Problems that occur at a given level of awareness can never be resolved at the same level of awareness. You need to raise your awareness to be able to witness clearly. With pure witnessing from a higher awareness, the problem no longer remains a problem. You begin to witness the beliefs and notions that are distorting your view, causing you to see it as a problem.

By being in Presence, you allow the problem situation to settle in the space of acceptance. You no longer resist it. You don't get into a discord. You remain in joyous harmony with the flow of whatever is happening. You remain aware of whatever *is*, without attaching any special meaning to it.

When you lend your detached presence through this way of witnessing, the solution emerges from the so-called 'problem' situation itself. If the solution demands action, you will then witness all the necessary actions *happening* through you or whoever else participates in the scene. No one remains to take credit for whatever happened by saying, "I did that."

You need to experience how solutions unfold from problem situations when you abide as the witnessing presence. This will build conviction in your nature as pure beingness.

3

The Fruit of Karma

Seeker 1: What determines the fruit of any action? Does the quality of action determine the fruit? Are there other factors?

Sirshree: The quality of action is determined by the Soul of Karma. If the Soul of Karma is awakened through love, wisdom and pure intention, then the action liberates you; it leads you to the ultimate fruit.

The fruit of any action is actually the internal state of mind. People believe that the fruit of action is achieved in the physical world. But the real fruit is your mental state.

Understand this with an example. There are two students, A and B, who are studying for their exams. 'A' studies very hard and scores 90% marks in the exams. 'B' does not study as hard as 'A' and scores 80% marks. What is the result of their karma?

Seeker 1: 'A' reaps the benefit of having studied hard. He scores more and enjoys the result. 'B' has to settle for lesser marks.

Sirshree: What if 'A' feels disappointed because he expected to score 95%? What if 'B' is jubilant because he didn't expect to score more than 70%? So we can see here that it is not the external result that matters. *The real result is the internal state of mind that follows. From this perspective, the fruit of karma can be only one of three possible outcomes – happiness, sorrow, or confusion.*

So, the result of action is determined by the thoughts and feelings that you entertain in response to situations, which in turn is determined by your understanding of life and its purpose.

Seeker 1: I seek clarity on that famous verse from the Bhagavad Gita, which states: 'Work without desiring the fruit of action.' What is wrong with desiring the fruit? Am I missing something in understanding this aphorism?

Sirshree: The Gita says: 'Perform your deeds without concerning yourself with the fruit of your deeds.' Taoism says: 'Act without expectation.' This does help to carry on with deeds without stumbling upon the block of negative emotions and feelings.

Expectation is one of the major causes of stress, disappointment, frustration, anger, irritation, depression, discouragement. When things don't happen as we expect them to happen and when people don't behave as we expect them to behave, such feelings arise.

When we are distanced from our true nature, we build expectations for the results of our actions. We seek instant gratification of desires, we expect people to respond positively, we wish for praise, approval, thankfulness, respect, recognition, and so on. When this doesn't happen, we sink into negative feelings.

Each one of our actions yields corresponding fruit. No one can escape action. Even if you do nothing all day and all night, you cannot escape its fruit because 'doing nothing' is also an action. Some results come instantly while others are delayed. Since many actions yield delayed results, people become frustrated or disappointed and stop performing these actions.

When we perform an action for the first time, our focus is on the action, because we don't yet know its result. We perform the action with intuitive thought, resulting in our best performance. *But as soon as we see the result of our action, our focus shifts to the result. We create an impression of the result in our mind. The next time we perform the same action, we hold onto our past impression of the result. Due to this, we do not act intuitively to the best of our ability.* The result is invariably different from the previous one, causing negative feelings.

Seeker 1: So we should not carry any expectations of the fruit of action because non-fulfillment can cause sorrow.

Sirshree: Yes. But that's not all. The irony is that expecting a particular result causes suffering not only when it remains unfulfilled, but also when it *is* fulfilled.

When the fruit is received as expected, it boosts the ego. The ego is reinforced with the belief that it can control the result. It also strengthens the focus on the fruit, rather than the action. This is a greater harm as it distances you from who-you-truly-are.

When expectations are fulfilled, the ego tries to fix the outcome of action and attempts to control the result. This causes stress while you perform action. Episodes of non-fulfillment become more painful.

Seeker 2: So this means that there is no point in keeping any expectation. Does it mean that we can't hope for anything at all while being engaged in action?

Sirshree: Forgoing expectations without completely understanding the truth fully in depth can lead to negative outcomes such as dullness and lack of purpose. It can also lead to misunderstandings. One may say, "How can I feel motivated to do something if I can't expect anything good in return?" Someone else may ask, "Should I work hard at my job but not expect a salary in return?"

Focusing on the result is inherently flawed and occurs due to ignorance of your true nature. You postpone your joy to the future attainment of the fruit. *True joy is never a result of action. Joy is your true nature. You cannot* do *something to* gain *joy. Rather the innate joy that is experienced in the awareness of who-you-truly-are naturally touches whatever you do.*

Joy is a quality of the Self. When you are in Self-awareness, you experience unconditional joy. You don't need to do something to gain happiness. Being alive, itself, becomes a cause for celebration. Inspired actions then happen through you, because you are experiencing the joy of aliveness.

If at all you do want to desire a fruit for your actions, then it can be said: *Perform your deeds and expect the ultimate fruit— Enlightenment—from the Source, not the channel.*

The aspiration for enlightenment will liberate you from all other desires. It will lead you to stabilize in the experience of the Self. Hence, if you want to expect anything at all, then desire the supreme fruit – Enlightenment!

Seeker 2: Thank you, Sirshree. This is a paradigm shift for me! We always act to attain happiness. It feels very relaxing to know that we can act from joy, instead of acting for happiness. What is the meaning of expecting from the Source and not from the channels?

Sirshree: You should expect the fruit from the Source, not the channel. The Source, here, means the Self, God, Consciousness. Expecting fruit from the channel only leads to disappointment. The channel is merely a channel; it is only the medium to deliver you the fruit. Suppose a person who lives in the desert visits you. Impressed with the water flowing through the taps, he says, "I will take a tap with me to the desert. Then we'll never face water scarcity again." What will you tell him?

Does the tap have any capacity of giving? The tap is merely a channel. There are many taps through which water is received, but they all come from the same water source. If you insist that you want water only from a particular tap, then you are inviting sorrow. If one tap closes, ten others can open for you. This is the way nature works.

Stop expecting the fruit from particular channels. Be open to receive the grace of the Source and rest in faith that the ultimate fruit will come from the Source through some channel at its right time.

In your daily dealings and interactions, know that you are giving to the Source and receiving from the Source. *You are dealing only with the Self. People are merely channels through which your interaction with the Self takes place.*

4

The Law of Karma

Seeker 1: I've been hearing and reading about the Law of Karma in various forums and literature. What exactly is the Law of Karma?

Sirshree: Let us look at some situations to understand the Law of Karma. Let us suppose young Sam stole from his father. He stole 100 rupees from his father's wallet. What, according to you, will happen by the Law of Karma? What does each one of you think? Let us start with you, since you asked the question...

Seeker 1: I think if Sam stole from his father, when Sam grows up, his son will steal the same amount of money from him.

Sirshree: What about interest? What if he does not get married at all? What do the rest of you think?

Seeker 2: Well, I believe that someone will steal from Sam. It could be money; it could be ideas. Nature will repay him someday.

And it need not be from a similar relationship. Nature can repay through anybody.

Seeker 3: I feel something wrong will happen to him and God will square off. It is not necessary that someone will steal. But for every 'debit', there will be a 'credit' in some form or the other to balance it out. Something bad will definitely happen to him.

Sirshree: So, do you think there is 'some one' to square off? Is there a divine accountant who keeps track of every karma?

Seeker 3: Yes, I believe so.

Seeker 2: Maybe nature keeps track. That is the law. Like the Law of Attraction, the Law of Karma has its effect and someone, somewhere keeps track.

Seeker 4: I believe this is all mere hearsay. Nobody keeps track. There is no impact of any karma. If one steals, one may enjoy the money. That's it. If he is caught stealing, he suffers. This is practical. This whole thing about Karmic retribution is unscientific.

Sirshree: Every answer here clarifies the beliefs you harbour. Let us change the question. In the story, what if young Sam apologizes to his father the next day? He confesses and returns the money. What do you think will then happen as per the Law of Karma?

Seeker 1: Someone will steal something from Sam when he grows up and will also confess to Sam.

Seeker 2: I agree with this answer. But it need not necessarily be when he grows up. It can be anytime.

Sirshree: So now, for something that Sam has done, someone will be made to not only steal, but also confess! Someone will go through all this, just to square off one person's karma? So then, this will set off a chain of square-offs, with no end!

Seeker 4: This is why I don't believe all this. Sam steals... he feels unhappy... he has got the result. Sam confesses... he feels happy... that's the next result. I don't see the need for anything beyond that.

Seeker 3: Well, if he confesses, then it is an altogether different thing. Then there is no impact of his Karma. Also, I have another idea. How 'young' Sam is also makes a difference. If Sam is a child, then it doesn't matter at all. There is no impact of his karma. But, if Sam does it knowingly, it will have a bearing on him.

I have a Jewish friend. He was telling me that the Jews believe that children are absolved off their karma. But they become responsible for their karma after they become teenagers. Till then, all actions are their parents' responsibility.

Sirshree: Yes. It is a Jewish custom to celebrate the *Bar Mitzvah* for children to signify their coming of age. Let us go back to the question and change the question further. What if Sam did not steal in the first place? What if he only thought about stealing? Would that be karma?

Seeker 1: No, merely thinking about stealing does not amount to karma, unless it manifests as external action.

Seeker 2: True. Karma means action. Thinking, by itself, is not "action" in the truest sense.

Seeker 3: I believe even a thought is karma. But, the impact of the karma will be lower. Perhaps someone will think of stealing from Sam. That's the only possible impact.

Seeker 4: Given that there is no major consequence of doing, I can't see why thinking can have any consequence. At the most, he may feel guilty about having entertained the thought of stealing. Or he may feel the sadistic joy in thinking about stealing. But ultimately it won't matter.

Scientifically speaking, a thought is just an electromagnetic impulse. It is too much to think that every electromagnetic impulse will have any consequence besides the impulse itself.

Sirshree: All very good answers. Now, consider with an open mind what the Law of Karma is, from a different perspective. *Consider that the only consequence of an action is that a 'tendency' is formed.* If Sam steals from his father, Sam forms a tendency of taking shortcuts. The consequence or fruit of this karma is that a pattern of taking shortcuts is ingrained in his subconscious mind. Or if this pattern is already there, this thought reinforces that pattern. Automatically, due to this pattern, Sam will attract situations in his life, where he will constantly seek easy shortcuts that may prove to be costly one day or the other. People will call this karma.

Seeker 4: So the result of his karma is the formation of tendency in his subconscious mind. How does repeated thinking lead to the formation of tendencies?

Sirshree: Understand this with an example. You would have seen streams flowing down the hills during the rainy season. These streams follow the same pathways in every monsoon. Why? Because the ridges that are carved by the constant flow of water become more deeply ingrained. When the water was flowing initially, it would have taken effort to clear the obstacles along the way. But later, these pathways provide the easiest ways to flow, as they offer no resistance.

Similarly, repeated behaviour becomes deeply ingrained as tendencies in the subconscious mind. Behaviour then tends to flow effortlessly along the routes of tendencies, as they have become habits. For example, when one tends to become angry, a habit of being short tempered is developed. As a result, man helplessly expresses anger even when he does not really want to.

Seeker 1: So, if I shout at someone today, the consequence of that karma is that my anger pattern becomes stronger.

Sirshree: Yes. And the pattern of anger becomes more deeply ingrained through the repeated expression of anger. Patterns are formed based on the intention that backs your action.

Let us understand the Law of Karma with one more analogy. There is a boy who thinks of cheating in his exams. He intends to copy from his notes. What, according to you, will be the impact of this Karma?

Seeker 1: Has he already decided to cheat in the exams or is he still hesitating?

Sirshree: Let us assume he is still contemplating. He thinks about it and then puts off the idea due to the fear of being caught or due to guilt that he is thinking something wrong.

Seeker 2: Based on what I've understood from you so far, the consequence of this karma is that his pattern of cheating and deceit will be reinforced by this thought.

Sirshree: Yes. Even 'thought' is karma. And then one day, he 'actually' cheats. He actually ends up copying from his notes in the examination hall because he has been thinking of doing it in the past. *So one consequence of his karma of thinking is that his tendency is reinforced and another consequence is that he may end up actually doing what he has been thinking about.* So, now tell me what is the consequence of his 'action' of cheating in the examinations?

Seeker 4: His subconscious mind begins to believe, "I am a cheat. I cannot do things in a straightforward way. I have to use deceitful means to succeed in life."

Sirshree: Right. So, the tendency is further reinforced. During the first instance, he brushes off the thought of cheating by considering that it is not the right thing to do. This is like drawing a line in water. It just causes some ripples. No significant consequence. It's just a fleeting thought. If he repeatedly thinks about it, it is akin to drawing a line on sand. The impressions remain for quite some time. If he actually cheats in the exams, it is like drawing a line on a rock with a hammer and chisel. The tendencies become extremely strong.

Seeker 3: So, depending on how deep this tendency has become, he may attract more incidents of cheating in his life.

Sirshree: Right. The possibility that someone will cheat him also increases. This is so because someone who cheats ends up attracting the company of others who cheat. So, the chances are that he will also be cheated in turn. He increases the experience of deceit in his life. He attracts things at the lower level of consciousness. If someone is corrupt, he begins to see more corruption than others. He may not only perpetrate more corruption, but also be at the receiving end of corruption in his own life.

Seeker 4: This is wonderful. This is scientific too.

Seeker 3: So if the Law of Karma is all about the tendency to repeat actions, does it mean that there is nothing like karmic retribution? What then is karmic bondage?

Sirshree: Firstly, it is important to remember that all actions originate at the mental level. Hence, karma is essentially mental action and the fruit of karma is also at the mental level. *Though actions and their results are manifest at the physical level, it is the mental karma in the form of thoughts and feelings that really matter.*

When actions are repeated in thought, they form subtle impressions on the subconscious mind. These patterns that are etched in the deeper mind are helplessly enacted. One becomes a victim to one's tendencies and manifests them helplessly. This is bondage.

Seeker 2: So again, karmic bondage is just about being bound to one's tendencies.

Sirshree: That is not all. The most important cause of karmic bondage is ignorance of who-you-truly-are. *Your true nature is pure consciousness; you are beyond the mind and body. However, when you are not aware of your true nature, you believe that you are a separate individual, limited to this body. The wave assumes that it is separate from the ocean. This is the original sin. Everything else that is popularly regarded as sin is just the cascaded effect of this original sin.*

Most spiritual practices deal with methods of eliminating secondary or derived sin – defilements like anger, hatred, fear, anxiety etc. These are the symptoms of the original sin. Merely working to resolve these symptoms cannot lead to liberation, as the original sin, the root cause, has not been dealt with. When we receive the understanding of our true nature and abide in it, we put an end to the root cause of all suffering.

Karma performed based on the assumed individual identity is sin. Karma that is based on the understanding of your true identity is the greatest virtue. Most often, actions are performed with a feeling of doership ("I did it"). We think, "I made this happen." Or "Oh! I shouldn't have done this; it's wrong." With such feelings, the individual egotistic 'I' is strengthened and we become bound to karma.

When we assume the limited body-mind as 'I', then it gives birth to the illusory notion of 'others'. This naturally gives rise to delusion, resulting in emotions like anger, fear, greed, hatred, envy, ill-will and resentment.

When we entertain such negative emotions in ignorance of our true nature, we actually resist the flow of life through our bodies. Negative, hurtful memories, bitterness, and ill-will choke the free flow of life within us. *When one holds onto grudges in life and feels bitterness and resentment, it clogs the free flow of life. Eventually this affects our physical wellbeing, causing chronic ailments in the longer term.*

By feeling resentment towards any person or situation, we actually plant seeds of hatred. We unknowingly place an order for even more resentment that rebounds back on us, multiplied many times over. We do this unknowingly due to lack of awareness. *With every act in our past where we have either felt hurt or caused others to feel hurt, we draw lines of bondage on the screen of pure consciousness. These lines of bondage block the free flow of life through us.*

When you resist the free flow of life, you experience testing circumstances, limitations and sorrow. Thoughts, feelings, words and actions that have arisen from the ignorant belief of separateness bind you and choke the expression of life. This is the manifest form of karmic bondage.

Actually, these limitations and sorrow come as wake-up calls to re-connect and re-align with the natural flow of the Self. They come as reminders to recognize and honour the essential Oneness of everything.

You need to get rid of these karmic bonds by performing actions that assert the truth of who-you-truly-are. This will open the doors to liberation from action. You will then effectively continue to perform the highest actions without incurring any karmic bondage.

Seeker 2: How can we get rid of these karmic bonds?

Sirshree: *People believe that they are performing the right karma when their externally visible speech and actions are positive and virtuous. However, feelings and the self-talk that goes on in the mind are also karma. Karmic bonds are formed at the mental level. Hence, karmic cleansing needs to happen essentially at the mental level.*

How do we get rid of karmic bondage? How do we free ourselves from the numerous difficulties of life and move towards total liberation? The answer: through the practice of forgiveness!

Forgiveness is not merely about seeking or accepting apologies; it has a deeper aspect to it. Forgiveness involves sensitivity, awareness, compassion and love. It completely wipes away hatred, resentment and ego and raises the purity and piousness of the mind. *Forgiveness is a conscious, deliberate decision to release feelings of resentment or vengeance towards anyone, even yourself. You surrender everything that has happened to the Self instead of arrogating it to yourself or others.*

True forgiveness involves letting go of deeply held negative feelings. It empowers you to recognize the pain you suffered without letting that pain define you, enabling you to heal and move on with your life. Forgiveness is actually an all-curing panacea that clears karmic bondages and enables divine love, joy and peace to flow in your life.

Every time you entertain impure or negative feelings for someone, a karmic line gets drawn on the whiteboard of pure consciousness, linking the two of you in a karmic bondage. Consciousness gets tainted with these impressions.

Since most people in the world are unaware of this law, they keep piling several such lines of bondage. As a result the universal consciousness that permeates the world becomes polluted, thereby obscuring its purity.

The complete practice of forgiveness consists of four aspects:

- Seeking forgiveness from people for negative feelings that you have harboured for them and any hurtful feelings that you may have caused them.
- Forgiving people for hurtful feelings that they may have caused you.
- Seeking forgiveness from your mind-body mechanism for knowingly or unknowingly favouring negativity, for neglecting and tormenting your own mind and body.
- Seeking forgiveness from the Source (God) collectively for yourself and on behalf of others.

If you practice this consistently with conviction from the bottom of your heart, not a single line of karmic bondage will remain on your whiteboard of pure consciousness. You will start experiencing divine love, joy and peace.

The best way to remain free from karmic bondage is to not create them. Raise your awareness to such a level that as soon as you get the slightest hint of negativity arising in your mind, you will instantly erase it by practicing forgiveness. But until you get to this level of alertness and awareness, you can start by erasing the karmic lines formed during each day at least every night.

You will also need to erase the several lines already drawn in the past on the whiteboard of consciousness. Even if a single line remains on it, then your liberation is at stake. While you cleanse karmic bondage of the past, you can raise your awareness to ensure that you do not draw any further karmic lines in the present.

Seeker 2: Thank you so much for this guidance. What you have said touches me deeply. I need to work on cleansing all the pent-up impressions from past incidents. I believe in the law of Karma because it helps me make sense of all the injustice in the world.

I have been taught since childhood that one is born poor or one is born with deformities because of his or her karma from past lifetimes. Isn't the law of karma also related to reincarnation?

Sirshree: The subject of reincarnation requires an elaborate discussion. Consider that reincarnation does not exist exactly in the way you believe it. We shall address this in further sessions.

5

The Question of Rebirth

Seeker: I have been told since childhood that we suffer in this lifetime due to our karma from past lifetimes. Is this true? Does reincarnation actually happen? Are we really reconciling our karma from previous lifetimes?

Sirshree: The question to be asked is: Who is actually born? Whose karma is it? Who is experiencing all this?

The belief in reincarnation arises when one is stuck with the limited perspective of the human body without understanding the grand game being played behind the scenes. The concept of rebirth is a fiction arising from the limited standpoint of individuality, of personhood. When one realizes the standpoint of the Self, of the universal consciousness, this question will lose its meaning.

Understand this with an analogy. Suppose you place your hand into a pot to feel the various things kept inside. As you put your hand in the pot, each finger touches a different thing. One of your fingers touches mud, another touches a flower petal. A needle pricks the third finger while the fourth finger feels the softness of cotton wool. Each finger gets a different kind of experience.

But, who is actually deriving the experience? Are these experiences limited to the fingers alone? No. It is for the one who has placed his hand in the pot to derive all these experiences. The one who is outside the pot receives all the experiences.

The fingers in this analogy represent human bodies. *Man feels that he is experiencing the various facets of life. But in reality, the Self, who is outside the manifest world, is the experiencer of everything. Whatever good or bad is happening, it is the Self, alone, who is receiving all those experiences.* The Self wishes to gather a diverse range of experiences through mankind.

Who is actually performing all karma through the human body? The Self, alone, is performing karma through all the bodies. And the Self, alone, is receiving the fruit of all karma.

Coming back to the analogy, the experiences that are gathered through the fingers are stored in memory. Suppose one of the fingers perishes. Consider that the hand grows another finger inside the pot. The one outside the pot re-uses the experiences of the perished finger from memory, and implants it in the new finger.

In other words, the experiences gathered by the Self through a particular body are available in the form of memories. *The Self re-uses memories gathered from one human lifetime by planting them in further bodies.*

When the individual (the finger) is unable to make sense of certain memories that are being played out during this lifetime, he believes that he has been reborn. He believes in the concept of reincarnation. *Actually, there is nothing like reincarnation. All incarnations are of the Self, alone. The Self is unborn. Yet it experiences birth through all bodies.*

Seeker: What is the purpose of re-using memories? What is the ultimate motive of the Self behind gathering experiences through mankind and re-using them?

Sirshree: The purpose of such re-use of memories is to bring about progressive evolution. The Self evolves through the re-use of experiences in subsequent bodies.

You can see that every new generation of man is ahead of the previous generation in terms of their level of understanding. This happens because the Self uses whatever experiences are gathered from a given generation to better the succeeding generations.

This is why you find that children of each generation are cleverer than their predecessors. Inventions in each generation have paved the way for further inventions in the generations that follow. You would have heard of child prodigies who demonstrate wondrous skills early in their childhood. There are three-year olds who can play the piano skillfully, children who are able to solve complex mathematical problems effortlessly. This demonstrates how the Self reuses memories of experiences drawn from previous bodies.

Through this process of progressive evolution, the Self explores its boundless potential. The Self reaches the pinnacle of its evolution– the state of Self-realization and expression of its divine qualities. One who does not know this game of the Self assumes it to be the rebirth of a previous human body. Man believes that he is evolving whereas, in reality, it is God who is evolving through each human form.

Seeker: Thanks for this perspective shift! It is so relieving to know that all the experiences are of the Self. All karma belongs to the Self. Even the fruit belongs to the Self. I have felt disappointed when denied help by friends whom I have helped. But now it is clear to me that I was entangled in the fingers, in the individualistic viewpoints.

Sirshree: Yes. When you identify yourself as a separate individual, you are troubled by the pricking experiences that come your way during this lifetime of your body-mind.

Man keeps grumbling that his life is filled with suffering. He keeps complaining: "Why me! Why am I going through such bitter experiences? I have helped my people, but no one helps me."

He should be asked, "Who are you?" The separate individual is only a notion. All the experiences are the Self's alone. If he helps his neighbour, it is like one finger helping its neighbouring finger. Upon Self-realization, clarity dawns that the hand is helping itself through the interplay of all its fingers! All help is Self-help.

When you are denied help, it is an opportunity to unconditionally express love. The opportunity is to learn, mature and evolve to a state where you realize yourself as the source of unconditional love and compassion.

Contemplate on this paradigm shift and build conviction in it. When one is convinced about this truth, one begins to live in devotion and marvel at this divine cosmic game.

6

Karma and Destiny

Seeker 1: Is it in our hands to shape our destiny? If God is deciding our destiny, then are we limited to achieve only as much as we are destined for?

Sirshree: What exactly is your concept of destiny? In whose hands is destiny? Who do you consider yourself to be? And who is God?

From the hand-in-pot example, you have seen that behind everything, it is God's hand alone. Everything is happening by His will – the Divine will. And by Divine will, the potential of your destiny encompasses everything in this universe and beyond!

People live with the limiting notion that "I get only as much as I am destined for." This notion is based on the core belief of scarcity. Many people believe in scarcity and entertain a feeling of lack. Such a belief leads to competition and an unconscious notion that you have to take away from others in order to get something. The belief of scarcity makes people feel that "If I have to win, others should lose."

The universe is teeming with unlimited possibilities. The world in which we live is wonderfully obliging. Everyone can win! *The supreme creative potential of the Self makes it possible to fulfill the wishes of everyone simultaneously. Allow 'faith in abundance' rather than 'fear of scarcity' to steer your life. There is abundance of everything for everyone.*

You are already destined for everything that you could possibly need in this lifetime. There is abundance of love, peace, bliss, health and wealth in your life and also everyone's life. There is a natural flow of money, time, happiness, and harmony in your life and everyone's life. You block this natural flow through your belief of scarcity.

You naturally progress toward your higher potential in life, so long as you do not place obstacles in the free-flow from the Self. This is the divine order of the universe.

The question to be asked is: "Will it be in my capacity to receive whatever I am destined for? How can I eliminate my negative feelings and limiting beliefs and harmonize with the free-flow of the Universe to fully receive whatever is in my destiny?"

Even if you were able to draw a minutest part of the infinite potential that you are destined for, what a life you would enjoy... A life brimming with love, joy, peace, wealth, health and creativity! You will be wonderstruck at what's in store for if you transcend your limiting beliefs.

When you realize who you truly are, when you realize your true nature as the immaculate Source of everything, your body will be too less to experience the sheer magnitude of bliss. You will say one body is not enough… you need more bodies to fully experience that bliss. You will begin to spread the joy. Thus, you will see that your destiny actually spans much beyond your individual needs to benefit many people.

Seeker 1: Thank you, Sirshree… I need to contemplate more on this shift in perspective. How do I free myself from past blocks that I have placed in the free-flow of my destiny?

Sirshree: *Every action that happens through you is like a seed that is planted in the field of consciousness. Consciousness is the field that nurtures and transforms these seeds into fruit.*

The Universe functions as a multiplier that multiplies the seeds that you sow. *Whatever you invest with the Universe is augmented multifold. The resulting harvest depends on the quality of the seeds that are plant.* The Multiplier works and multiplies all the seeds irrespective of whether they are from a beggar or the emperor. Everything you give, comes back, multiplied.

It is very important to be happy when you plant the seeds through your actions. *Feelings are the real seeds that you plant while acting. Your external action is not as important as the internal feeling that you are in. The seeds of your feelings germinate and bring respective results.* Positive feelings provide immense positive charge to the seeds. You can do nothing about the blocks that have been created in the past. *Your future is governed by the seeds of feeling that you plant today, by the feelings that you choose in every situation that you encounter each day. Don't plant weeds of sorrow; plant seeds of happiness in the present.*

Develop the habit of frequently asking yourself, "Am I planting seeds or weeds? Am I singing in harmony or grumbling in discord?" This will help in raising your awareness of your feelings. If you find that you are not attuned to the divine flow, you can attune yourself through such questioning.

Whatever we give, comes back to us multifold. This is the law of the universe. Give your best to the Best to get the best. Sow the best seeds. This is the key to consistent and sustainable growth.

A farmer is well versed with this principle. He knows the importance of sowing the best seeds. After planting the best seeds, he tends to his fields, provides them water, nourishment and care, and leaves the rest to the Universe. Once the harvest is ready, he collects the crop and again segregates the best seeds from the harvest for re-plantation. The best seeds are planted again to improve the harvest. In this way, the quality of the seeds and the harvest keeps growing continuously.

This is the secret of infinite growth. Learn and familiarize yourself with this secret. Sow the best of your seeds. When results manifest, you receive a multifold of what you had given. Again from the new gifts you've received, re-plant the best ones in the Universe to get even higher quality of results. This is Faith in Action.

Seeker 2: My friends say that wearing gemstones or energetically harmonizing my house with *Fengshui* can bring good luck. Is this true?

Sirshree: Due to ignorance of the Divine law of abundance, many people live with false notions. Some say, "You will gain only if you work hard," others say, "Wear these good luck charm or this lucky gemstone and your fortune will change for the better."

You only need to learn the art of planting healthy seeds through the right thoughts so as to bring forth the grandeur that you're destined for. It is your thoughts that contribute the most into determining your life. The feeling that you live in shapes your life. When people find their life changing by using good luck charms or gemstones, *Fengshui* or *Vaastu*, it is largely the change in their beliefs that works to bring about the change in their fortune.

Those who are bound by a victim-mindset tend to believe in the vagaries of whatever their sun-signs or horoscopes foretell. When you go beyond a mechanical way of living and perform conscious karma, then astrological readings no longer bind you. There is no question of being lucky or unlucky, happy or unhappy. Who-you-truly-are is the source of luck, the wellspring of happiness.

Seeker 2: Why do problems appear in our life? Why do we run into troublesome people and difficult circumstances from time to time? Am I planting the wrong seeds through negative thoughts? Is there any way I can find why certain undesirable events are happening in my life?

Sirshree: Problems can be the result of karmic bondages. The way to eliminate karmic bondages is to practice forgiveness from the bottom of your heart.

However, there is more to this. Those seemingly problematic people and circumstances in your life can also be the result of your prayers. *If you have prayed for self-progress, nature throws difficulties at you so that you can develop the qualities necessary for overcoming those difficulties.*

Human life is all about developing qualities and reaching one's highest possibility. The divine plan of everybody on earth is to progress to his or her highest potential and express all that they have developed. If you are aligned with your divine plan, you need to take each problem as a challenge.

Let every situation remind you that it has come for your higher progress. Everything that is happening in life is for your growth and to bring completeness. Remembering this will help you tide through rough situations with ease and perseverance.

You need to harbour positive feelings for the people and situations that pose problems. It is easy to get angry, hateful and bitter at them. By doing so, you are planting weeds for your future. But remember that they have arrived in your life to help you, not harm you. When you remember this, you will receive every circumstance gracefully without grumbling.

Seeker 2: At times, it is difficult to maintain my composure. An unhappy feeling grips me. As you said, my actions are rendered negative, leading to planting of negative seeds.

Sirshree: *Unhappiness is actually a hint from nature, which indicates that you have strayed away from the happy natural state of who-you-truly-are. This is a marvelous system that works infallibly.*

Whenever you sense that your feelings are becoming negative, you are not feeling nice, it only means that you are not in harmony with the natural flow of the Self. *You can consider the feeling of unhappiness as God's way of reminding you to return to your happy natural state.* In that sense, unhappiness can be considered as an invitation to return to the blissful state of pure awareness.

Consider that the thoughts that you are entertaining or the way you are acting is against your true nature. Nature automatically hints at this by giving you an unhappy feeling. This is also known as the power of conscience. By raising your sensitivity and awareness you can take corrective steps by shifting your focus to your blessings, to the unconditional grace that is flowing in life.

7

Transcending the Three Temperaments

Seeker 1: We find people with different dispositions. Some are very active, always engaged in action, while there are others who are sedentary. What drives their dispositions? Is it true that some people are subject to more karma, while others aren't?

Sirshree: Human behaviour is governed by three tendencies – *Sattva*, *Rajas* and *Tamas*. These three *gunas* (qualities, temperaments) determine the tendencies of the human body-mind. The play of these three temperaments is subtle and unseen, but their symptoms are perceivable at all levels of human existence – physical, mental, intellectual and occupational.

Tamas is the tendency of inertia or passivity. *Rajas* is the tendency of motivity or activity. *Sattva* is the tendency of equanimity or balance. The proportion of these three temperaments within the human body-mind shapes its overall behaviour. This is why you find people prone to a variety of dispositions.

Tamas is characterized by lethargy, inertia, passivity, ignorance, greed and attachment to lowly desires. Tamasic people tend to eat stale food; they don't like fresh and lively food. They are laid-back and find solace in pleasures that stimulate their senses. A tamasic body is prone to lethargy. A tamasic mind indulges in base thoughts and negative emotions like hatred, anger, ill-will. A tamasic intellect is dull and rigid.

Rajas is a temperament that fuels activity. It serves as an engine for life-in-action. However, when this engine gets into overdrive, the result is hyperactivity. Rajasic people find it difficult to relax, both physically and mentally. They have to be constantly engaged at work. They just cannot stay still. They prefer hot and spicy food. They are highly ambitious, whether or not they have the qualities to achieve them. They are rarely satisfied with whatever is, and constantly seek new sensations and variety in life.

Sattva is the quality of equanimity and balance. It is the most subtle and intangible of the three gunas. Sattva provides composure, level-headedness, purity and virtuousness. Sattvic people are sensitive to the effects of food on the body and mind. They always eat well-balanced and optimum amount of food. Sattvic people make optimum use of sleep, activity and rest. They do not overindulge in any one thing. They tread the middle path. Sattvic people can be in a state of rest even while working, because they have learnt the art of relaxed action.

It is possible to have a mix of these tendencies at various levels of existence. For example, one who has a predominantly tamasic body can have a predominantly rajasic mind. Such a person will always be lost in incessant thinking and emotional sways while being physically sluggish.

Seeker 2: I've read about the merits of being Sattvic. It is said that being in equanimity is true yoga. I need to strive to become sattvic.

Sirshree: Everyone would love to become sattvic after getting to know its virtues. It is very much in our power to increase the temperament we want. All the three gunas are present in everyone in different proportions. It's not that sattva is totally absent in tamas or rajas predominant people. Some amount of sattva is alive even in the most tamasic or rajasic people. It's just that it has been muted because such people have constantly ignored it in favour of tamas or rajas. Constantly ignoring the sattvic force within your body-mind makes it dormant.

The secret to develop sattva is to program your subconscious mind with habits that promote sattva. You can begin with your eating habits. An oft-repeated saying is that you are what you eat. Program your mind to enjoy easily digestible, nutritious and energizing food. Avoid heavy, fatty, spicy, sugary, processed and preserved food.

When you begin with reforming the habits of your body, your mind too will follow suit. When we begin from the bottom and move upwards, we automatically receive cues from nature regarding what to do next. Act upon the cues and develop sattvic habits. Soon enough, you will find yourself enjoying a sattvic lifestyle.

However, here's a word of caution. *Being sattvic is not the ultimate goal of life. There are dangers of remaining stuck with the sattvic way of life without seeking to go beyond it.*

Seeker 2: I was of the opinion that equanimity can help in stilling the mind and being in the experience of Self. How could being sattvic be dangerous? And what is beyond equanimity?

Sirshree: *To be able to understand the state beyond Sattva, you need to first understand that these gunas are temperaments of your body, mind and intellect; they are not your qualities. You are not your body, mind or intellect.* Your essential nature is consciousness, the Self. The Self presides over the body, mind and intellect. *You are not a pawn in the hands of your gunas; you are the master of your gunas. It is you who needs to take control of them and not the other way round.*

The state that is beyond the three gunas is known as the *Gunateet* state – the state that transcends these temperaments of your body-mind mechanism. *Being in the Gunateet state, you can make use of the three gunas as and when you require them for Self-expression, without being susceptible to their influence.*

Many people who take to spirituality consider the progression to the Sattvic way of life as the final goal. There are dangers inherent in resting on the plateau of Sattva, without transcending it.

The biggest danger of remaining stuck with sattva is the probability of backsliding into tamas. If sattvic people are unaware that there is something beyond sattva, they can become complacent, egoistic and arrogant.

Seeker 2: But people of sattvic nature perform selfless deeds for the good of others. Doesn't this contribute to their progress?

Sirshree: There is no harm in doing selfless service, as long as they are truly selfless. People of Sattvic nature tend to take credit for performing altruistic deeds for the wellbeing of society. True wisdom lies in surrendering all deeds to the Self. However, they revel in a sense of self-pride for being the doer of noble deeds.

Being bound by negative karma is like being bound to iron handcuffs. However, being attached to virtuous deeds is like being bound to golden handcuffs. Even if they are golden, they are handcuffs after all… they bind you. One cannot easily discern this subtle form of bondage. While avoiding negative karma is good, being attached to positive karma can stall your progress. Sattva-predominant people need to progress, by transcending both – negative and positive karma.

'I know it all' is a very dangerous belief. *People who have the arrogance of 'I know it all' can get trapped in the mire of Sattva. They tend to be lost in intellectual delights and flaunt their knowledge of spirituality. Such knowledge is mere information, not true wisdom.* True progress happens only when one becomes empty off all notions and abides like an empty flute, through which divine music can be played.

It can be considered unfortunate for someone who has come near the ultimate state to then backslide due to complacency or arrogance. It would be sad because this person had overcome tamas and rajas and had the momentum to transcend the gunas.

Seeker 1: We see most people aspiring for a balanced life and limit themselves to virtuous actions. This is indeed a revelation that merely being virtuous and balanced can also be risky. How is this state that transcends the three temperaments?

Sirshree: Pure Consciousness is the state that transcends the three temperaments. In this state of conscious presence, you choose when to use tamas, when to use rajas and when to use sattva.

Being in the gunateet state your gunas are at your discretion. For example, at bedtime, you make use of tamas to get into deep sleep. While meditating you make controlled use of tamas and sattva to enter into deep state of stillness. When some activity needs to be done, you make use of rajas and perform the activity. Thus, for everything that you need to do, you have your gunas at your disposal.

The gunateet state is a state of Self-stabilization. You don't need external motivation to lead life in this manner. If the need is to get up and do something, you simply activate the rajas guna and start doing it. You are aware that you are employing the guna for the divine purpose of your body-mind; hence you don't get attached to it. You experience yourself as the detached witnesser of all activity. You recognize that you are not defined by your gunas. You clearly see your gunas as mere tools. You choose your tools; the tools don't choose you. You make a wise decision every time because you are not swayed by your temperaments. This is true Self-mastery.

The gunateet state doesn't distance you from the world. You take part in every activity that you need to. Inspired actions arise from the Self and express through your body-mind. You connect and transact with the world, but you are not attached to it. You have a top-view of things. You express divine love for people; not 'personalized' love that is related to the body and mind. Every activity becomes a means of Self-expression instead of fuelling the ego.

Seeker 1: I can see that I am often tied down by the grip of tamas. I escape action and prefer to follow the path of least resistance. I can strive to raise myself to a sattvic life. But is it ever possible for me to attain such an exalted state that you've described?

Sirshree: It is possible to attain this state, because it's already available within you. If it had to be acquired from elsewhere, then it wouldn't have been possible. You need to raise your level of consciousness by listening to the truth, through service unto the truth, through devotion of the truth.

Begin by raising your awareness to spot the play of the temperaments. Notice when tamas dominates your choices. Observe where rajas takes you away from the state of relaxed alertness. Be vigilant about how the ego bloats about sattvic qualities. With heightened awareness, you will be able to spot when tamas, rajas and sattva are at work in your body-mind.

For example, consider the situation when you decide to sit in meditation. If you are sattva-predominant, you will immediately sit in meditation. Spot the rise of tamas or rajas here. If you feel like resting or procrastinating, tamas is at work. If you feel like watching your favourite TV show or doing some work or activity, rajas is at work. Watch the play of temperaments unrelentingly, while abiding in the experience of conscious presence.

You need to raise your awareness so that you not only move from tamas to sattva, but also transcend sattva into the stateless state of the Self.

8

Enlightenment through Conscious Karma

Seeker 1: How do I progress towards enlightenment? There are various paths that are popular in the scriptures. Which path is more effective?

Sirshree: *There are many paths that lead to stabilization in Self-experience, such as Gyan (Wisdom), Dhyana (Meditation), Karma (Action), Japa (Chanting), Self-Enquiry, Bhakti (Devotion), etc. But they can broadly be divided into just two – the Path of Wisdom and the Path of Devotion.*

The Path of Devotion is the path of surrender to the divine will of God. It is the path of submitting to Consciousness–the Source of everything. Effort in this path is effortless, as actions happen in joyous surrender to the Self.

The Path of Wisdom is that of will power, where the seeker of Truth applies his intellect to grasp the Truth and internalize it.

The Path of Devotion is akin to a kitten, which leaves its body loose and gives itself up to its mother, who then carries it around with her mouth. The Path of Wisdom is like that of a baby monkey that needs to clasp onto its mother's belly when she jumps from one branch to the other. The kitten surrenders. The baby monkey clutches with all its might.

All the paths that are known in spirituality finally culminate in this two-fold path – one approach is that of complete surrender, while the other is that of intellectual reasoning and meditation. The seeker of Self-realization needs guidance on both these paths.

Seeker 1: So do both these paths lead to the same result?

Sirshree: Understand this with the help of an example. There were two travellers who needed to cross safely through a jungle to return home. One of them was blind, while the other did not have legs. Individually, they could not have made it home. The lame traveller climbed onto the shoulders of his blind companion and started guiding him through the jungle. The blind man followed his directions and walked carefully, carrying him through the jungle and both managed to reach home safely.

So it is on the path of Self-realization. The lame man symbolizes the eye of wisdom, while the blind one represents the legs of devotion. Without the legs of devotion, the eyes of wisdom cannot walk the path. And the legs of devotion cannot see the path without the eyes of wisdom. Let devotion obtain the eyes of wisdom and let wisdom in turn receive the legs of devotion.

The seeker who pursues the path of wisdom through the practice of meditation and conscious karma develops unswerving faith, thereby leading to the surrender of his individual personhood to the Self. The

one who follows the path of devotion matures in understanding of the Truth. Finally the one who works on gaining wisdom surrenders and the one who surrenders attains wisdom. Thus, both the paths merge at its culmination in Self-realization.

Tejgyan *is that understanding that culminates these paths - those on the path of wisdom attain devotion and those on the path of devotion attain wisdom.*

Seeker 1: So then, how do I start? Which path do I choose to start the journey?

Sirshree: With Tejgyan, you begin directly with the understanding that brings together both Wisdom and Devotion. You do not have to decide which path is best for you. Whatever the mind prefers need not be the best path for you. Following the path that the mind feels like is like asking a thief how he would like to be captured. The thief would never give away the path that would lead to his downfall. Similarly, the aspect of the mind that considers itself as a separate individual has to drop. That aspect of the mind cannot be trusted to decide which path to tread. Leave how this happens to grace. Ultimately, grace is the only way.

Seeker 2: I have read about Karma-yoga in the Bhagvad Gita. Since I am working in the industry, wouldn't the path of right karma be the most appropriate for people like me?

Sirshree: In essence, there are only two paths – wisdom and devotion. Both, Karma-yoga (the path of right action) and Dhyana-yoga (the path of meditation) are essentially the practice of wisdom.

Karma-yoga is not actually a path. It is the practice of conscious

action backed by higher understanding. It is wisdom-in-action. The seeker applies effort to transmute higher understanding into action.

The corporate world or any other chosen occupation is merely a field of activity that serves the higher purpose of Self-realization and Self-expression. *Functioning in your chosen field of activity serves you to discover your true nature, build conviction in it and to be established in the experience of your true nature. Conscious action in all facets of your life propels you towards this ultimate aim behind all the aims that you pursue.*

The practice of conscious action slowly shifts the earnest seeker from doing into being. *With consistent practice of conscious action, one begins to increasingly abide in conscious presence. In this state of detached being, beyond doing and non-doing, one simply witnesses actions arising as the spontaneous play of happening.* Through the practice of abiding in this state, the notion of separateness dissolves and actions become a cause for liberation.

Seeker 3: I've known of many people who take a break from industrious life and take to the practice of meditation. Isn't meditation a more effective way of transcending action and resting in pure consciousness?

Sirshree: The practice of Dhyana (Meditation) has been grossly misunderstood as that of inaction. This is a missing link. Meditation is the state of being absorbed in Self. Meditation is your essential nature. *When viewed as the state of being in Self-awareness, meditation has nothing to do with doing or non-doing. It is not an escape from the world. One can be engaged in action while being absorbed in the state of Self-meditation.*

The term, Meditation, is also used to refer to the practice that leads to this state. Meditation, when viewed as this practice, is a way of stilling the mind. The mind tends to indulge in thoughts of the world. Incessant thinking becomes a habit. It is a compulsive dis-ease, as it keeps you away from the state of complete ease. The practice of meditation helps you detach from thoughts that plague your awareness. It raises awareness of pure consciousness.

The daily practice of meditation is a preparation to connect with the world in the right way. It prepares you to abide in awareness of Self, while being engaged in worldly activity.

Seeker 3: Thank you, Sirshree. This helps to clarify that I need not withdraw or take a break from activity to practice meditation. Since you said that the practice of meditation prepares one to connect with the world in the right way, does it mean that the practice of meditation precedes the practice of right karma?

Sirshree: Just as the paths of wisdom and devotion are complementary, one naturally leading to the other, similarly the practice of meditation and right karma are complementary too. One naturally leads to the other.

Meditation can be viewed as a double-headed arrow. While your focus is directed on the world and its affairs, this very focus on the world serves to illumine the knowing presence. The light of awareness, which illumines everything that is being known, reflects on itself. Awareness becomes aware of itself.

The more you dwell in the state of meditation on Self, it serves as a thinner to weaken your attachment to the mind's notions, beliefs, and tendencies. The habit of identifying with personality is weakened. You remain absorbed in pure consciousness – the very light in which everything arises and subsides.

Being absorbed in the Self automatically transforms your action. Your actions become increasingly non-personalized, arising from the immaculate standpoint of totality. Actions happen not from the notion of 'doing', but from the essence of 'being'. In this way, meditation translates into inspired action.

However, the converse is also true. *The practice of conscious action backed by higher understanding naturally leads the seeker into a meditative state. When actions are performed in the remembrance of the Self, one rises beyond doing and non-doing.* Detached witnessing gains precedence. While actions happen through the body-mind, the detached witnessing presence becomes increasingly prominent. *Every action is an opportunity, an invitation to honour the divine presence that enlivens it.*

Meditation is like downloading a media file in offline mode for later viewing. Meditation is practiced by being in the stillness of presence. You cleanse your past conditioning by allowing it to rise into your awareness and watching it as a detached witness.

The practice of conscious karma is like online streaming video. You watch the video in real-time as it is being downloaded. In the same way, *the practice of conscious karma happens in and through your daily interactions in the world. You cleanse your mind of past conditioning by encountering it through your interactions with the world.* Every situation, every incident serves as an opportunity to practice conscious karma.

Thus, the one who delves into the depth of Self-meditation naturally begins to manifest inspired actions arising from the non-personal standpoint of the Self. And the one who acts by abiding in constant remembrance of the Self naturally begins to settle into inner stillness of Self-meditation.

Since both meditation and karma are aspects of the Path of Wisdom, both ways, finally culminate in devotion.

Seeker 3: This is wondrous! We can start anywhere and we'll naturally reach the same destination of the Self.

Sirshree: Yes. *Ultimately, the experience that karma, devotion, meditation and wisdom lead to is one and the same. Performing karma in the spirit of wisdom is true devotion.* Performing awakened action in the light of recognition of the Self is devotion.

Seeker 1: Wow! This statement encompasses all the so-called paths – karma, wisdom and devotion. Gratitude for this, Sirshree! Till today, I have been reading and believing them to be separate paths, but now I am beginning to see how these three are integrally one.

Seeker 2: What is the crux of the practice of karma-yoga?

Sirshree: Karma means action. Yoga means uniting. Thus, karma-yoga is the practice of uniting with the Self through the practice of conscious action.

The Self alone is the living reality. The individual personality that you assume as 'I' is merely an idea, a notion. Mere intellectual understanding of this does not suffice. You know about the Truth;

but you need to live it. Karma-yoga is about consciously living this understanding. Let this understanding permeate all actions.

In essence, it is about surrendering all action and the fruit thereof to the Self. It is the state of being in action, where there is neither doing nor non-doing. Neither do you do, nor do you refrain from doing. You watch actions happening through your body-mind with the understanding that the Self is enlivening all activity.

Seeker 2: There are situations when we are in no mood to act. There are also testing circumstances where we are held by anger or engulfed by disappointment. How do we abide by the practice at such times?

Sirshree: Can you cite an example from your own experience?

Seeker 2: When I am not able to cope with work pressures, my tasks remain incomplete. When my boss criticizes me in team meetings, I feel his comments are often nasty and demoralizing. I feel in no mood to continue working on such days. This reflects even in my family, as I tend to carry this mood home. I vent my frustration on my wife and son for no fault of theirs.

Sirshree: Emotions can cause you to withdraw into a shell and avoid appropriate action. You feel paralyzed and lose the impetus to perform actions that are appropriate in your field of work.

Emotions can also force you to react impulsively in situations where keeping peace and patience is the apt response. By force of habit, you may feel compelled to retort angrily at your family when being peacefully responsive is appropriate at home.

This happens because you identify with emotions. You believe that they're happening with you. Emotions arise in the body due to past conditioning. They arise based on programmed interpretation of events, your thoughts, people's behavior, the weather, and body sensations.

How you handle the sway of emotions depends on your level of awareness in the given situation. If you are able remain aware and be detached, then you can use the play of emotions to remember and honour who-you-truly-are.

Emotions, whether pleasurable or painful, are happening with the body. Pure consciousness is the untouched knower of these. You are this Pure Consciousness. If you are able to keep distance from the emotions, you can continue to perform deeds that are apt for the given context by remembering that these emotions are with the body, not with who-you-truly-are.

When you are able to take a pause and access the experience of conscious presence, you clearly recognize that these emotions are temporary. They come and go. They are like clouds floating in the expansive sky of awareness. You will then observe emotions as a detached witness.

When you consciously witness the feeling of sorrow or anger, the truth of these emotions is revealed. When you bring conscious presence into your witnessing, you no longer resist the emotion. The emotion then serves to reveal your true nature as pure awareness.

Seeker 2: Thank you. I will practice daily meditation to abide in pure awareness, so that I can practice in the midst of testing circumstances. But sometimes, the situations are very difficult to detach from. Keeping distance from the situation becomes difficult. Is there a way out when I am tangled in feelings? How do I maintain awareness during such episodes of emotional flux?

Sirshree: *Situations are never difficult. Situations are what they are. The emotions that arise within you make it appear to be difficult. You only need to handle your emotions.*

There can be times when you are attached with the scene and consumed by emotions. At such moments, it may seem difficult to detach from the body-mind and connect with the experience of pure awareness. At such junctures, you can practice to loosen the grip of emotion by surrendering the emotion to the Self.

Conscious action is not just about surrendering your actions. It is also about surrendering emotions that arise within you. Remind yourself that God alone is. Everything is happening in the light of consciousness. Surrender every happening, every emotion and every action to the Self. If you happen to impulsively react, then surrender that reaction also to the Self.

If time permits, spend time in shooting prayers. Immerse yourself in a deep sense of prayer for liberation from the pull of emotions and tendencies. Use the intensity of the emotion constructively and transmute it into an equally strong prayer for liberation.

When you have surrendered the experience of emotions to the Self, it has a stilling effect on the mind. The mind, that was restless, settles down and is able to take relevant and suitable action in the given context.

Seeker 3: Please elaborate on relevant suitable action. How do we decide what action is relevant or suitable?

Sirshree: Taking relevant suitable action despite negative feelings that restrain you is an important aspect of the practice. When emotions cloud you, it may seem difficult to determine how to act.

Anger may compel you to retort in situations where maintaining silence may be beneficial. It is in anger that many people use such words or commit such deeds, the effects of which are often irrevocable. Abusive words or acts of violence expressed in anger are then followed by feelings of guilt and regret.

Similarly, boredom is another feeling that can compel you to act in order to bring some change in your state of mind. When the current state of mind is non-palatable and unexciting, the mind seeks avenues for excitement and indulges. *When you watch the feeling of boredom in a detached manner without giving in to it, it can reveal many hidden aspects of your mind. The joy of freedom from compulsive behaviour is far more superior to the pleasures that one seeks by escaping boredom.*

Depression, sorrow, resentment or any other form of resistance to circumstances can prevent you from acting by what your role demands. When emotions pull you back, you can find the way by asking yourself the right question. Ask yourself: "What would I have done, had this incident or situation not happened?" Acting unconditionally, just as you would have done without the negative feeling, is suitable action. Action, that arises after dipping into the stillness of conscious awareness, is inspired action.

Consider a little child who's down with gastric disorder and cannot take in food. However, the mother eats her meals regularly. Some may feel that she's being selfish to feed herself when her poor child is unable to eat anything. But if you look deeper, you'll find that she has to feed herself and keep fit, so that she can take care of her child.

This is an example of performing relevant and suitable karma despite negative feelings. The mother's act of having timely meals embodies her love for her child. Although she may not feel like eating when her little child is going without food, she understands that she should tend to herself so as to be able to care for her child. Her behaviour is based on a benevolent intention.

This also shows that karma cannot be judged by external manifestations. It is the Soul of Karma, comprising love, pure intention and understanding that determine its quality and end-result.

Seeker 4: Very often, I don't feel like getting into activity when I am back home from my workplace. I feel tired and hence prefer to take rest. Is this avoidance of suitable karma? Am I not tending to my body by taking rest?

Sirshree: Even mental or physical fatigue is a condition that constrains actions that could perhaps still be possible. Most people often tend to give a blanketed statement that they are tired and give up any possibility for action. When they declare that they are tired, the body, which is listening to these words, also gives up and slumps down on the bed.

When you declare that you are tired, examine exactly which parts of the body are fatigued. Are the eyes tired? Is the back sore?

Are the hands tired? What is the exact sensation in those parts of the body? Let your awareness touch those parts that are stressed. This will relax and rejuvenate them.

Seeker 4: Thank you. I am beginning to realize that I should consciously observe whatever feelings or sensations arise and act despite them.

Sirshree: Yes. *Allow consciousness to flow into your actions. Acting from pure awareness despite being engulfed by limiting emotions is true devotion. Devotion is not just about singing praises; it is about consistently choosing a higher response despite being gripped by conflicting feelings.* The word 'despite' is the key in *sadhana* (spiritual practice).

Firmly resolve to act by whatever is suitable and relevant to the given situation despite constraining feelings, despite differences with people, despite a disagreeable weather, despite any painful memories that may arise. True devotion is practiced by acting unconditionally despite all odds in remembrance of the divine presence. This is true love. Be in love with God through surrender, through unconditional actions.

Seeker 1: Being in love with God... Is this the same as being the experience of the Self?

Sirshree: *Either be in the experience of God, or be in love with God.*

The experience of Self-awareness is a state of Oneness, where Self alone is. In this state, everything serves merely as a mirror that illumines the Self. This is the state of Self-realization in which you need to be stabilized.

However, if you find yourself aloof from the experience of Self-awareness, then be in the feeling of devotion. *Work becomes worship when it is imbued with an attitude of service to the Self. Act from love for the living presence that enlivens all this. Work with an impersonal attitude and surrender the act to the Self.*

Either be in the experience of God, or be in love with God. Be certain that you abide in one of these two states. When one is not in one of these states, then the judgmental mind entraps you. You are consumed by stories and emotions of the mind and lose the touch of divinity.

Always remember to either BE the Ocean or SEE the Ocean. Either abide in the experience of God or keep your focus attuned in the love of God.

You can send your opinion or feedback on this book to :

Tej Gyan Foundation, Pimpri Colony, P. O. Box 25,
Pimpri, Pune – 411017 (Maharashtra), INDIA
email : mail@tejgyan.com

About Sirshree

Sirshree's spiritual quest which began during his childhood, led him on a journey through various schools of thought and meditation practices. His overpowering desire to attain the truth made him relinquish his teaching job. After a long period of contemplation, his spiritual quest culminated in the attainment of the ultimate truth. Sirshree says, **"All paths that lead to the truth begin differently, but end in the same way—with understanding. Understanding is the whole thing. Listening to this understanding is enough to attain the truth."**

Sirshree is the author of several spiritual books. His books have been translated in more than 10 languages and published by leading publishers such as Penguin and Hay House. He is the founder of Tej Gyan Foundation, a not-for-profit organization committed to raising mass consciousness by spreading "Happy Thoughts" with branches in the United States, India, Europe and Asia-Pacific. Sirshree's retreats have transformed the lives of thousands and his teachings have inspired various social initiatives for raising global consciousness.

His works include more than 100 books and 3000 discourses. Various luminaries and celebrities such as His Holiness the Dalai Lama, publishers Mr. Reid Tracy and Ms. Tami Simon and yoga master Dr. B. K. S Iyengar have released Sirshree's books and lauded his work. 'The Source' book series, authored by Sirshree, has sold more than 10 million copies in 5 years. His book *The Warrior's Mirror*, published by Penguin, was featured in the Limca Book of Records for being released on the same day in 11 languages.

Tejgyan... The Road Ahead

What is Tejgyan?

Tejgyan is the existential wisdom of the ultimate truth, which is beyond duality. In today's world, there are people who feel disharmony and are desperately trying to achieve balance in an unpredictable life. Tejgyan helps them in harmonizing with their true nature, the Self, thereby restoring balance in all aspects of their life.

And then there are those who are successful but feel a sense of emptiness or void within. Tejgyan provides them fulfillment and helps them to embark on a journey towards self-realization. There are others who feel lost and are seeking the meaning of life. Tejgyan helps them to realize the true purpose of human life.

All this is possible with Tejgyan due to a very simple reason. The experience of the ultimate truth is always available. The direct experience of this truth is possible provided the right method is known. Tejgyan is that method, that understanding. At Tej Gyan Foundation, Sirshree imparts this understanding through a System for Wisdom – a series of retreats that guides participants step by step

Magic of Ultimate Awakening Retreat

Magic of Ultimate Awakening is the flagship self-realization retreat offered by Tej Gyan Foundation The retreat is conducted in two languages – Hindi and English. The teachings of the retreat are non-denominational (secular).

This residential retreat is held for 3-5 days at the foundation's MaNaN Ashram amidst the glory of mountains and the pristine beauty of nature. This ashram is located at the outskirts of the city of Pune in India, and is well connected by air, road and rail. The retreat is also held at other centres of Tej Gyan Foundation across the world.

Participate in the *Magic of Ultimate Awakening* retreat to attain ageless wisdom through a unique simple 'System for Wisdom' so that you can:

1. Live from pure and still presence allowing the natural qualities of consciousness, viz. peace, love, joy, compassion, abundance and creativity to manifest.

2. Acquire simple tools to use in everyday life which help quieten the chattering mind, revealing your true nature.

3. Get practical techniques to access pure presence at will and connect to the source of all answers (the inner guru).

4. Discover missing links in practices of meditation *(dhyana)*, action *(karma)*, wisdom *(gyana)* and devotion *(bhakti)*.

5. Understand the nature of your body-mind mechanism to attain freedom from tendencies and patterns.

6. Learn practical methods to shift from mind-centred living to consciousness-centred living.

For retreats contact +919921008060 or email: mail@tejgyan.com

About Tej Gyan Foundation

Tej Gyan Foundation (TGF) was established with the mission of creating a highly evolved society through all-round self development of every individual that transforms all the facets of his/her life. It is a non-profit organization founded on the teachings of Sirshree. The foundation has received the ISO certification (ISO 9001:2015) for its system of imparting wisdom. It has centres all across India as well as in other countries. The motto of Tej Gyan Foundation is 'Happy Thoughts'.

TGF is creating a highly evolved society through:

- Tejgyan Programs (Retreats, Courses, Television and Radio Programs, Podcasts)

- Tejgyan Products (Books, Tapes, Audio/Video CDs)

- Tejgyan Projects (Value Education, Women Empowerment, Peace Initiatives)

TGF undertakes projects to elevate the level of consciousness among students, youth, women, senior citizens, teachers, doctors, leaders, organizations, police force, prisoners, etc.

MaNaN Ashram

Survey No. 43, Sanas Nagar, Nandoshi gaon,Kirkatwadi Phata, Sinhagad Road, Dist. Pune 411024, Maharashtra, India.

Books can be delivered at your doorstep by registered post or courier. You can request for the same through postal money order or pay by VPP. Please send the money order to either of the
:following two addresses
. WOW Publishings Pvt. Ltd
Registered Office: E-4, Vaibhav Nagar, Near Tapovan . 1
.Mandir, Pimpri, Pune 411017
Post Box No. 36, Pimpri Colony Post Office, Pimpri, , Pune .2
411017
Phone No. : 9011013210 / 9623457873

:You can also order your copy at the online store
www.gethappythoughts.org
.-/Free Shipping plus 10% Discount on purchases above Rs. 300*

For further details contact:

Tejgyan Global Foundation

Registered Office:
Happy Thoughts Building, Vikrant Complex, Near
Tapovan Mandir, Pimpri, Pune 411017, Maharashtra, India.
Contact No: 020-27411240, 27412576
Email: mail@tejgyan.com

MaNaN Ashram:
Survey No. 43, Sanas Nagar, Nandoshi gaon, Kirkatwadi Phata,
Sinhagad Road, Tal. Haveli, Dist. Pune 411024, Maharashtra, India.
Contact No: 992100 8060.

Hyderabad: 9885558100, **Bangalore:** 9880412588,

Delhi: 9891059875, **Nashik:** 9326967980, **Mumbai:** 9373440985

For accessing our unique 'System for Wisdom' from self-help to self-realization, please follow us on:

	Website	www.tejgyan.org
You Tube	Video Channel	www.youtube.com/tejgyan For Q&A videos: http://goo.gl/YA81DQ
facebook	Social networking	www.facebook.com/tejgyan
twitter	Social networking	www.twitter.com/sirshree
	Internet Radio	http://www.tejgyan.org/internetradio.aspx

Online Shopping
www.gethappythoughts.org

Pray for World Peace along with thousands of others at 09:09 a.m. and p.m. every day

www.ingramcontent.com/pod-product-compliance
Lightning Source LLC
LaVergne TN
LVHW040158080526
838202LV00042B/3225